1001 EXCUSES FOR EVERYDAY LIFE

The Ultimate Guide to Getting Out of Anything!

BY LOREN MOTOYAMA

Printed in the United States of America
ISBN: 979-8-234-09685-2

Acknowledgements

To my parents, Howard and June — who raised me, believed in me, and led by example every single day. They never gave me excuses, and they never accepted any of mine. This book is proof that it stuck.

And to my daughter Morgan, who proofread every page with a dedication that puts most of these excuses to shame. She had no excuse not to — and she delivered. Any errors that remain are entirely her fault. (They're not. She was wonderful.)

Introduction

We've all been there. That awkward moment when you realize you forgot a birthday, missed a call, skipped out on a commitment, or just needed a reason — any reason — to get out of something. Excuses have been part of the human experience since the dawn of time. From students dodging homework to adults avoiding family functions, the art of the excuse has evolved right along with us. Some excuses are believable, some are wildly creative, and some are so outrageous they just might work.

1001 Excuses for Everyday Life: The Ultimate Guide to Getting Out of Anything! is a playful collection of alibis, reasons, and justifications for life's many situations. Inside, you'll find fifty categories covering everyday mishaps, social dilemmas, academic scrambles, workplace blunders, and everything in between. Each category includes a blend of serious, plausible excuses alongside a handful of humorous, over-the-top explanations for those moments when honesty needs a little help — or when you're just in the mood for a laugh.

This book isn't here to encourage bad habits or help you dodge responsibility forever (well… maybe just a little). It's a lighthearted celebration of the excuses we make, the creativity behind them, and the situations that turn all of us into excuse-makers from time to time. Whether you need a quick save, a clever line, or a laugh-out-loud moment, this collection has you covered. Use it responsibly — or at least confidently. Now turn the page, and let the excuses begin.

Table of Contents

Table of Contents

CHAPTER 1

Excuses for Being Late to Work

SERIOUS EXCUSES

1. Traffic crawled after a wreck on my usual route.
2. My car wouldn't start; I had to wait for a jump.
3. My kid's drop-off took longer than expected.
4. A freight train blocked the crossing for ages.
5. I had to help a family member before I left.
6. My alarm went off, but I hit snooze too often.
7. A last-minute work email kept me at home.
8. Construction detoured me miles out of the way.
9. I spent too long searching for my keys.
10. I started late because I didn't sleep well.

HUMOROUS EXCUSES

1. I was abducted by aliens and they dropped me off late.
2. My GPS insisted I take the scenic route.
3. I was stuck in an epic battle with my alarm clock.
4. My coffee mug held me hostage until I filled it properly.
5. I got trapped in a philosophical debate with my mirror.
6. I had to rescue my breakfast from burning.
7. My shower decided to perform an opera this morning.
8. My car and I had a disagreement about leaving.
9. A squirrel made direct eye contact with me and I had to wait it out.
10. My driveway refused to let me back out until I apologized for something.

CHAPTER 2

Excuses for Missing School

SERIOUS EXCUSES

1. I woke up with a fever and stayed home.
2. My parent had an emergency and needed help.
3. The school bus never showed up this morning.
4. A migraine made it hard to even get dressed.
5. I had to watch my younger sibling unexpectedly.
6. We had car trouble and couldn't get there in time.
7. I had a doctor's appointment we couldn't reschedule.
8. I felt too sick to concentrate or sit in class.
9. A family issue came up late last night.
10. My ride forgot they were supposed to pick me up.

HUMOROUS EXCUSES

1. My dog ate my backpack.
2. I was recruited by a marching band passing by.
3. My bedroom door jammed and I was trapped inside.
4. A time traveler borrowed my homework.
5. I thought it was Saturday.
6. My backpack and I had a falling-out over its organizational system.
7. I was trapped in a video game tutorial.
8. My alarm clock and I had an irreconcilable difference of opinion.
9. The front door sensed my reluctance and kept swinging back open.
10. A butterfly landed on my shoe and the moment felt too important to interrupt.

CHAPTER 3

Excuses for Forgetting a Birthday

SERIOUS EXCUSES

1. I mixed up the date in my calendar.
2. I was juggling too many deadlines and lost track.
3. My phone reminders didn't sync correctly.
4. I focused on a family issue and everything else blurred.
5. I remembered early in the week and then spaced it.
6. I wrote it down on a sticky note I misplaced.
7. I thought the celebration was next weekend.
8. I kept meaning to call and the day slipped away.
9. I confused your birthday with someone else's date.
10. I relied on social media to remind me and it didn't.

HUMOROUS EXCUSES

1. My calendar app developed amnesia.
2. I wrote it on my hand in pen and then washed my hands like a responsible adult.
3. My brain filed it under "next year's problems."
4. I thought you were turning timeless.
5. I was hypnotized into forgetting.
6. My watch stopped at yesterday.
7. I assumed birthdays were becoming quarterly events.
8. My brain double-booked that memory slot with a song I can't stop humming.
9. I asked my houseplant to remind me and it let me down.
10. The birthday fairy skipped my notification list this year.

MEETING
IN
PROGRESS

CHAPTER 4

Excuses for Skipping a Meeting

SERIOUS EXCUSES

1. I had a conflicting appointment I couldn't move.
2. A client call ran long and overlapped the meeting.
3. I joined the call on time but had the camera and mic off and didn't realize it.
4. My internet went down right before it started.
5. A task I expected to take ten minutes turned into a two-hour detour.
6. I never saw the updated meeting invitation.
7. I joined the wrong link and realized too late.
8. I was in transit and couldn't get to a quiet spot.
9. A coworker needed immediate help with a problem.
10. I thought my attendance was optional, not required.

HUMOROUS EXCUSES

1. My coffee maker double-booked me.
2. My office chair staged a counter-meeting and I attended that instead.
3. My Wi-Fi router sent me the wrong virtual meeting link.
4. I thought "meeting" meant "meditation."
5. My GPS rerouted me to the donut shop.
6. I was busy refereeing a soap opera plot twist.
7. My calendar app pranked me with fake alerts.
8. I prepared a seventeen-point agenda and no one told me the meeting was canceled.
9. I was waiting for the meeting to come to me.
10. My mouse froze, and I interpreted it as a vote from the universe.

CHAPTER 5

Excuses for Not Calling Back

SERIOUS EXCUSES

1. I saw your call while I was busy and then forgot.
2. My phone was on silent for most of the day.
3. I listened to the voicemail but got pulled into work.
4. I meant to call that evening and fell asleep.
5. I assumed I'd see you in person and delayed calling.
6. My battery died and I lost track afterward.
7. I had family over and didn't step away to call.
8. I got anxious about the conversation and stalled.
9. I was driving when you called and couldn't respond.
10. I kept waiting for a better time that never came.

HUMOROUS EXCUSES

1. My phone went into hiding.
2. I was trapped in a staring contest with my toaster.
3. I thought telepathy was working fine.
4. I was waiting for Mercury to leave retrograde.
5. My ringtone hypnotized me into silence.
6. I gave my phone a spa day.
7. My voicemail became self-aware and screened calls.
8. Every time I opened the app, someone else called and I had to start the whole process over.
9. I rehearsed the call so many times it felt like I'd already had it.
10. My phone kept showing me dog videos and I lost all sense of time.

CHAPTER 6

Excuses for Being Late to a Date

SERIOUS EXCUSES

1. Parking near the place took much longer than I expected.
2. I underestimated how long getting ready would take.
3. Traffic near the restaurant suddenly backed up.
4. I had to fix a wardrobe issue before leaving.
5. My ride-share took a long detour.
6. A last-minute family call delayed me.
7. I got turned around looking for the location.
8. I set out on time but doubled back twice because I couldn't remember if I'd locked the door.
9. I spilled something and had to change clothes.
10. I was nervous and kept second-guessing my outfit.

HUMOROUS EXCUSES

1. My mirror gave me fashion advice for an hour.
2. I got lost in my own neighborhood.
3. My shoes refused to cooperate.
4. I was stuck in a rom-com marathon in my head.
5. My reflection wouldn't let me leave until I smiled.
6. I mistook the time zone.
7. My confidence needed a pep talk.
8. I took a wrong turn and ended up in a neighborhood that looked more interesting.
9. My navigation app guided me through every pothole in the city first.
10. I stopped to let a family of ducks cross and they were very slow decision-makers.

CHAPTER 7

Excuses for Avoiding a Party

SERIOUS EXCUSES

1. I was completely drained after a long week.

2. I started feeling sick that afternoon.

3. My anxiety spiked about being in a big crowd.

4. A family situation popped up and needed me there.

5. My ride canceled and I couldn't get another.

6. I had an early start the next morning.

7. I got caught up helping a neighbor with an issue.

8. I misjudged how much work I still had to finish.

9. I wasn't feeling like myself and didn't want to drag it out.

10. The weather turned bad and I stayed home.

HUMOROUS EXCUSES

1. My couch handcuffed me.

2. My pajamas staged a rebellion against real clothes.

3. I was in witness protection from karaoke.

4. I thought it was a costume party and panicked.

5. My social battery needed charging.

6. I was teaching my goldfish to dance.

7. My streaming queue filed an injunction.

8. My horoscope specifically told me to stay home that night.

9. I started getting ready and accidentally fell into a documentary.

10. My cat sat on my coat and I couldn't ethically move her.

CHAPTER 8

Excuses for Not Doing Homework

SERIOUS EXCUSES

1. I left the assignment folder at school.
2. I misread the due date and thought it was later.
3. I spent forty-five minutes looking for a pencil and lost all momentum.
4. I helped a sibling with their work instead.
5. I got stuck on a question and didn't ask for help.
6. My laptop crashed and I lost what I'd done.
7. I had practice and came home worn out.
8. I had to babysit and couldn't focus.
9. I forgot the online login information.
10. I didn't understand the instructions and froze.

HUMOROUS EXCUSES

1. My pencil went on strike.
2. I turned it into origami.
3. My textbook developed writer's block.
4. I thought a streaming marathon was the assignment.
5. My pencil case opened, assessed the situation, and closed again.
6. Aliens beamed it up.
7. My brain declared homework-free Friday early.
8. My eraser kept undoing all my progress and I gave up.
9. My desk lamp pointed directly at my eyes the whole time and I couldn't see a thing.
10. My chair became suspiciously comfortable right at homework time.

CHAPTER 9

Excuses for Not Cleaning the House

SERIOUS EXCUSES

1. I ran out of the one cleaning product that makes the whole process feel worthwhile.
2. Work ate up more of the day than I planned.
3. We had last-minute visitors and I never started.
4. I spent the day running necessary errands.
5. I had to focus on one urgent room only.
6. My back was acting up when I tried to tidy.
7. I cleaned one room thoroughly and declared it a moral victory for the day.
8. I prioritized cooking over cleaning this time.
9. I helped someone else with their emergency instead.
10. I looked around, got overwhelmed, and stalled.

HUMOROUS EXCUSES

1. My broom went on strike.
2. I was testing new interior design: chaos chic.
3. My vacuum ran away with the mop.
4. I thought cobwebs were seasonal decorations.
5. My house declared independence from cleanliness.
6. I was waiting for the mess to become vintage.
7. I thought a little chaos built character.
8. I found a very old magazine and suddenly it was three hours later.
9. The dust gave me a look that said it was happy where it was.
10. I made a cleaning playlist and spent so long choosing songs that it got too late.

CHAPTER 10

Excuses for Forgetting to Buy Groceries

SERIOUS EXCUSES

1. I drove past the store and only remembered later.

2. I got distracted by another errand on the way.

3. I thought we still had enough at home.

4. I forgot my list and decided to wait.

5. I was exhausted and went straight home.

6. The store was packed and I couldn’t face the line.

7. A family call kept me on the phone while I was out.

8. I misjudged how quickly we’d run out of food.

9. I focused on one item and forgot the rest.

10. I planned to go after dinner and then crashed.

HUMOROUS EXCUSES

1. My shopping cart developed commitment issues.

2. I thought groceries would deliver themselves.

3. My fridge said it wasn’t hungry.

4. I mistook the store for a library.

5. My shopping list was classified by the government.

6. I thought we were fasting this week.

7. My shopping list became invisible.

8. I drove to the store but a good song came on and I kept driving.

9. My stomach forgot to remind me until we were already home.

10. I made eye contact with the shopping cart and felt no spark.

CHAPTER 11

Excuses for Missing a Deadline

SERIOUS EXCUSES

1. I underestimated how long the work would take.

2. I ran into problems I didn't foresee.

3. Another urgent project jumped ahead in priority.

4. I was waiting on information from someone else.

5. I misread the due date by a day.

6. I tried to perfect details instead of finishing.

7. I lost part of the file and had to redo it.

8. I got sick and fell behind for a few days.

9. I didn't speak up when I was overloaded.

10. I spent too long on smaller tasks first.

HUMOROUS EXCUSES

1. The deadline sprinted faster than I did.

2. My coffee mug swallowed my notes.

3. I lost the file in a parallel dimension.

4. My calendar mistook it for April Fool's Day.

5. My deadlines had a secret meeting and moved without telling me.

6. My progress bar hit 99% and just stayed there for three days.

7. My procrastination skills were too advanced.

8. My calendar had one job and it failed us both.

9. I sent the work ahead mentally, so technically it was there.

10. My productivity was stuck in beta and never fully launched.

EVENT

CHAPTER 12

Excuses for Not Showing Up to an Event

SERIOUS EXCUSES

1. I started feeling really ill that afternoon.
2. My childcare fell through at the last minute.
3. My ride gave me the wrong address and by the time I sorted it out it was over.
4. I had a sudden work call that ran long.
5. I confirmed the date twice and somehow still arrived twenty-four hours early.
6. My ride had an emergency and canceled.
7. The weather turned dangerous and I stayed home.
8. I had a spike of social anxiety and froze.
9. I didn’t realize how far away the venue was.
10. I got stuck dealing with a home repair issue.

HUMOROUS EXCUSES

1. My couch staged a sit-in.
2. I was invited to wizard academy orientation instead.
3. My GPS staged a protest and rerouted me home.
4. I was stuck in an endless group text.
5. I got trapped in an email thread debating whether the event was still happening.
6. I was waiting for my clone to finish getting ready.
7. My motivation got stuck in traffic.
8. My body started walking toward the door but my brain vetoed it.
9. I got dressed, sat down to rest, and woke up two hours later.
10. I got completely ready, sat down to put my shoes on, and simply never stood back up.

CHAPTER 13

Excuses for Running Out of Gas

SERIOUS EXCUSES

1. I misjudged how far I could go on the light.

2. I skipped stopping because the station looked busy.

3. I thought prices would be better at the next exit.

4. I didn't realize how remote that stretch of road was.

5. I kept saying "I'll get it after the next turn."

6. The gauge has been unreliable and I trusted it.

7. I was rushing and didn't want to add a stop.

8. I forgot my wallet and couldn't fill up earlier.

9. I changed routes and didn't pass any stations.

10. I lent the car out and didn't check afterward.

HUMOROUS EXCUSES

1. My car went on a hunger strike.

2. I thought the car ran on optimism and good vibes.

3. My car believed it was solar-powered.

4. I mistook "E" for "Excellent."

5. My fuel gauge was playing hide and seek.

6. I bribed my car with good intentions instead of fuel.

7. My car wanted to diet before beach season.

8. My car and I had a gentleman's agreement and it broke its end.

9. I was convinced the needle was stuck and the tank was actually fine.

10. I passed eleven gas stations hoping the twelfth would have better vibes.

RENT

CHAPTER 14

Excuses for Being Late Paying Rent

SERIOUS EXCUSES

1. My paycheck cleared later than expected.

2. I misread the due date on the lease.

3. An unexpected bill wiped out my balance.

4. I was waiting for a transfer to go through.

5. I thought I'd already scheduled the payment.

6. I mixed up which account the rent comes from.

7. I had to cover a sudden family expense first.

8. The online portal kept rejecting my payment.

9. I didn't notice the reminder email in time.

10. I relied on auto-pay and it failed this month.

HUMOROUS EXCUSES

1. My bank account filed for emotional asylum.

2. I spent it all on "emotional support pizza."

3. A magician made my money disappear.

4. I invested everything in invisible socks.

5. My financial philosophy is "pay it forward" — specifically, forward to next month.

6. A fortune teller told me it was a free month.

7. My money went on vacation without me.

8. My wallet asked for more time and I respected its boundaries.

9. I thought about paying it so many times it started to feel like I already had.

10. My checkbook and I were in a cooling-off period.

CHAPTER 15

Excuses for Oversleeping

SERIOUS EXCUSES

1. I stayed up way too late the night before.

2. My alarm volume was turned down too low.

3. I set the alarm for PM instead of AM.

4. My phone died overnight and never rang.

5. I took a sleep aid and it hit harder than expected.

6. I'd been sleep-deprived all week and crashed.

7. I forgot to switch my alarm back after a day off.

8. I snoozed too many times and drifted off again.

9. A storm knocked out power and reset everything.

10. I thought I'd wake up on my own and didn't.

HUMOROUS EXCUSES

1. My bed had me in a headlock.

2. I was competing in an extreme nap competition.

3. My dream wouldn't let me leave.

4. I mistook the alarm for background music.

5. Gravity kept me pinned to the mattress.

6. My blanket whispered "five more minutes."

7. My alarm and I have an understanding: it suggests, I advise, neither of us commits.

8. I set four alarms in the confidence that future me would handle it. Future me did not.

9. My pillow filed paperwork to keep me there until noon.

10. My body clock was still running on last weekend's timezone.

CHAPTER 16

Excuses for Forgetting an Important Task

SERIOUS EXCUSES

1. I never wrote it down anywhere.
2. I wrote it on three different surfaces and then cleaned all three of them.
3. I misjudged how many things I could juggle.
4. My reminder was set for the wrong day.
5. I left the notes somewhere I didn't check.
6. I assumed I'd remember without a list.
7. I underestimated how tired I'd be by evening.
8. I mixed it up with another deadline.
9. I focused on smaller tasks and overlooked the big one.
10. I was distracted by bad news that day.

HUMOROUS EXCUSES

1. I remembered it perfectly at 2 a.m. and assumed that would be enough to carry it to morning.
2. I gave it a sticky note in my head — my head ate the sticky note.
3. My memory card was full.
4. My reminder app sends notifications I have trained myself to dismiss without reading.
5. My to-do list became self-aware and hid.
6. I thought mind-reading would remind me.
7. I was so proud of remembering it once that I stopped putting in any further effort.
8. It fell off my to-do list and landed somewhere unreachable.
9. I delegated it to a version of myself that never showed up.
10. I put it at the top of my mental list and my mental list immediately filed it under "someone else's problem."

CHAPTER 17

Excuses for Not Answering the Door

SERIOUS EXCUSES

1. I was in the shower and didn't hear it.
2. I had headphones on and missed the knock.
3. I thought it was a delivery I didn't need to sign.
4. I wasn't dressed appropriately to come to the door.
5. I was on a sensitive call and couldn't step away.
6. I didn't recognize the person through the peephole.
7. I was elbow-deep in a project and stopping felt like it would cost me an hour of focus.
8. I was in the back room and heard it too late.
9. I thought it was for the neighbor, not me.
10. I was trying to calm a crying child.

HUMOROUS EXCUSES

1. I thought it was the pizza guy with my neighbor's order.
2. I was in witness protection from the cookie squad.
3. I mistook your knock for a drum solo.
4. I was rehearsing my ninja stealth routine.
5. My doorbell rang in Morse code, and I needed translation.
6. I was busy building a pillow fort.
7. I made accidental eye contact through the peephole and then had to commit to the bit.
8. I was in the middle of a very convincing impression of someone who isn't home.
9. My doorbell has cried wolf too many times and I stopped believing it.
10. I was in the middle of a very important snack.

P

CHAPTER 18

Excuses for Forgetting Where You Parked

SERIOUS EXCUSES

1. I rushed in and didn't note the section.
2. I used a different entrance than usual this time.
3. I was distracted by my phone as I walked in.
4. I assumed I'd remember the row and didn't.
5. I parked in a hurry to make it on time.
6. The lot was nearly full and everything looked the same.
7. I changed levels and forgot which one.
8. I left through a different exit than I entered.
9. I didn't pay attention to the landmark near my car.
10. I parked farther away than usual and lost the spot.

HUMOROUS EXCUSES

1. My car entered stealth mode.
2. I parked in an alternate dimension.
3. I parked with total confidence and walked away like a person who would definitely remember that.
4. My mental map of the lot was extremely detailed and completely wrong.
5. My car insisted on playing hide-and-seek.
6. My brain's parking module was running on dial-up.
7. I parked so well it became invisible.
8. Every car in the lot was conspiring to look the same.
9. My phone's parking reminder sent itself to spam.
10. I chose a creative spot and it was too creative to locate again.

CHAPTER 19

Excuses for Forgetting a Name

SERIOUS EXCUSES

1. We were introduced quickly and I didn't register it.
2. I was focused on what I was about to say.
3. I met several people at once and mixed them up.
4. I recognized the face more than the name.
5. I heard it over background noise and missed it.
6. I didn't repeat the name out loud to lock it in.
7. I haven't seen you often and it slipped my mind.
8. I confused your name with someone else I know.
9. I was nervous and barely heard introductions.
10. I stored it mentally in the wrong context.

HUMOROUS EXCUSES

1. My brain replaced your name with "Captain Awesome."
2. I know your name lives somewhere in my brain; I just can't find the folder it's in right now.
3. I renamed you in my head and forgot your actual name.
4. I thought you were incognito.
5. My brain auto-corrected you into another person.
6. I remember your face, your laugh, your dog's name, your birthday — just not yours.
7. My memory bank was experiencing technical difficulties.
8. My brain swapped your name for a pasta shape and I couldn't undo it.
9. The moment I knew it, someone said something louder and it fell out.
10. I introduced you to someone else and in that moment I truly could not hear myself speak.

WEDDING

CHAPTER 20

Excuses for Not Attending a Wedding

SERIOUS EXCUSES

1. I couldn't afford the travel and hotel costs.

2. A close family member scheduled surgery that week.

3. I had a non-refundable commitment already booked.

4. My passport or ID issue wasn't resolved in time.

5. I couldn't get the time off approved at work.

6. A major family event fell on the same date.

7. I started feeling seriously ill right before the trip.

8. My childcare options fell through for the whole weekend.

9. I was eight months pregnant and couldn't travel.

10. I was dealing with a heavy personal situation.

HUMOROUS EXCUSES

1. I was allergic to wedding cake that day.

2. My tuxedo staged a rebellion.

3. I was asked to be best man at Bigfoot's wedding.

4. My GPS insisted I attend a divorce party instead.

5. My alarm clock thought vows were optional.

6. I was still RSVP-ing in Morse code.

7. My dancing shoes went into hiding.

8. My formal wear sensed the occasion and panicked.

9. I RSVP'd yes in pencil, and it faded.

10. A competing life event showed up uninvited and won.

CHAPTER 21

Excuses for Not Walking the Dog

SERIOUS EXCUSES

1. The weather turned unsafe with ice and strong wind.
2. I wasn't feeling well enough to go out.
3. I worked later than expected and got home exhausted.
4. I let the dog play in the yard instead.
5. I thought someone else in the house had taken him.
6. I got caught up in a call and lost track of time.
7. I had to clean up a mess inside first.
8. My back or knee pain flared up.
9. I kept delaying until it was too dark.
10. I ran out of time before an evening commitment.

HUMOROUS EXCUSES

1. My dog refused to sign the walking contract.
2. The leash ran away without us.
3. My dog insisted on watching TV instead.
4. I was out-negotiated by the cat.
5. The dog was practicing telepathy, not walking.
6. My dog made a face at the weather that said this wasn't happening without a compelling argument.
7. I was waiting for my dog's permission slip.
8. My dog looked at the weather, looked at me, and went back to bed first.
9. The leash and I were not on speaking terms that evening.
10. My dog started a petition to relocate the walk to tomorrow.

CHAPTER 22

Excuses for Forgetting to Lock the Door

SERIOUS EXCUSES

1. I thought I'd locked it on my way out.
2. My hands were full of bags and I forgot to check.
3. Someone else left after me and I assumed they would do it.
4. I stepped out for a moment and didn't recheck.
5. I was running late and rushed through the routine.
6. I locked the top deadbolt but forgot the knob.
7. I got a phone call right as I was walking out the door.
8. I rely on habit and it failed me that time.
9. I thought the auto-lock had engaged on its own.
10. I popped back inside for something and forgot to lock it on the way out.

HUMOROUS EXCUSES

1. The lock told me it wanted freedom.
2. I thought my security system was psychic.
3. I mistook the knob for a handshake.
4. I wanted burglars to feel welcome.
5. My door was protesting curfews.
6. I hired an imaginary bouncer instead.
7. I was testing my neighborhood's honesty.
8. I triple-checked it in my head the entire drive and somehow that felt equivalent to actually checking.
9. My hand reached for the lock but a phone notification derailed everything.
10. I was so proud of myself for leaving on time that I forgot everything else.

CHAPTER 23

Excuses for Forgetting to Pay a Bill

SERIOUS EXCUSES

1. I thought I'd set it on auto-pay.
2. The reminder email got buried in my inbox.
3. I logged in to pay it, got distracted by an unrelated account balance, and closed the app.
4. My bank card expired and I didn't update it.
5. I was waiting for a statement that never arrived.
6. I assumed my partner had taken care of it.
7. I had to wait until I got my next paycheck.
8. I set it aside to handle later and forgot.
9. I misread the notice and thought I had more time.
10. I paid other urgent expenses first and lost track.

HUMOROUS EXCUSES

1. I paid with play money by mistake.
2. My wallet ran off to Vegas.
3. A magician vanished my checkbook.
4. I set it to auto-pay, which I now realize I only did in my imagination.
5. I thought "bill" referred to my uncle.
6. My bank account went on a diet.
7. I was waiting for my money tree to bloom.
8. I opened the app, got distracted by its other features, and never came back.
9. My bank sent a reminder and I accidentally starred it instead of acting on it.
10. The bill and I agreed to pretend it didn't exist for one more week.

CHAPTER 24

Excuses for Not Renewing a License

SERIOUS EXCUSES

1. I didn't even know my license had an expiration date!
2. I kept meaning to schedule an appointment.
3. I didn't realize the office closed earlier that day.
4. I assumed the reminder letter would come and didn't.
5. I put the renewal notice in a pile and lost it.
6. I forgot to bring the required documents.
7. I moved and wasn't sure where to renew.
8. I thought I still had a grace period.
9. I tried to pay it online but the website wasn't working.
10. It was the longest line I've ever seen, so I left to make an appointment instead.

HUMOROUS EXCUSES

1. I was waiting for a license fairy to deliver it.
2. I thought my license had nine lives.
3. A wizard told me I was immortal and didn't need one.
4. I believed my smile alone was valid ID.
5. I was testing life in the "pirate driver" lane.
6. I didn't realize "expired" meant they actually stop working.
7. I can't get a new license — have you seen my current photo? I look amazing.
8. I assumed good behavior extended the expiration automatically.
9. The DMV website looked at me and I looked at it and neither of us blinked first.
10. My license asked for one more year together and I caved.

INSTRUCTIONS

CHAPTER 25

Excuses for Not Following Instructions

SERIOUS EXCUSES

1. I skimmed them too quickly and missed details.
2. I thought I already knew the process.
3. I didn't realize there was a second page.
4. I misinterpreted one step and it threw me off.
5. I was embarrassed to ask for clarification.
6. I followed an older version of the directions.
7. I jumped in before reading everything all the way.
8. I got interrupted halfway through and lost my place.
9. I confused these instructions with another task.
10. I didn't see the update that changed the steps.

HUMOROUS EXCUSES

1. My GPS was giving me life directions instead.
2. The instructions self-destructed like in a spy movie.
3. I thought "follow directions" meant "take a walk."
4. My brain hit shuffle mode.
5. I was saving the instructions for bedtime reading.
6. I thought they were written in ancient hieroglyphs.
7. My creativity overruled the instructions.
8. The instructions were in a font that made them look optional.
9. I read step one so confidently that I assumed the rest would be similar.
10. I read them, felt confident, set them down, and proceeded based entirely on vibes.

CHAPTER 26

Excuses for Skipping Chores

SERIOUS EXCUSES

1. I was exhausted from work and needed a break.
2. I spent longer than planned on errands.
3. I had to help someone else with their project.
4. My back started hurting when I tried to start.
5. I had a headache and couldn't face scrubbing.
6. Everything took twice as long as I expected.
7. I thought I'd get to it after dinner and didn't.
8. I focused on one big task and ignored the rest.
9. I had to prepare for an early morning instead.
10. I got pulled into a long phone conversation.

HUMOROUS EXCUSES

1. My vacuum formed a union and walked out.
2. The dust bunnies demanded independence.
3. I was conducting a scientific dust collection experiment.
4. I was waiting for the house elves to show up.
5. My living room floor declared itself a relaxation sanctuary.
6. I thought chores were just suggestions.
7. I started a pro/con list for cleaning and spent the rest of the evening refining the con column.
8. The chores and I agreed to a temporary ceasefire.
9. I told myself I'd do it after this one thing and that one thing had several chapters.
10. My cleaning supplies locked themselves in the closet in protest.

CHAPTER 27

Excuses for Forgetting a Password

SERIOUS EXCUSES

1. I haven't logged in for ages and it slipped my mind.
2. I changed it recently and never memorized it.
3. I mixed it up with another account's password.
4. I relied on a notebook I couldn't find.
5. I stored it in a password app I can't access.
6. I used a pattern that I no longer remember.
7. I reset it once and forgot the new version.
8. I was in a rush and didn't write it down.
9. I didn't realize the system required a special character.
10. I tried too many guesses and got locked out.

HUMOROUS EXCUSES

1. Hackers stole my memory, not my account.
2. I used "password" but forgot the extra "s."
3. I set it as Morse code and lost the key.
4. I thought "12345" was universal.
5. My brain auto-saved it in invisible ink.
6. I made it so secure that even I can't get in — which technically means it's working.
7. My security questions became too secure.
8. I made it too clever and outsmarted myself.
9. My password manager forgot it too, so really we're both victims here.
10. I changed it to something unforgettable and immediately forgot it.

RESTAURANT

CHAPTER 28

Excuses for Not Making Dinner Reservations

SERIOUS EXCUSES

1. I assumed we'd get a table without booking.
2. I thought you preferred something more casual.
3. I kept meaning to call and ran out of time.
4. I misread the date of when we needed it.
5. I couldn't decide on a restaurant and stalled.
6. I checked once, saw it was busy, and gave up.
7. I forgot to confirm after checking availability.
8. I thought you were handling the reservation.
9. I planned to book it at lunch and got swamped.
10. I didn't realize how popular that place had become.

HUMOROUS EXCUSES

1. I sent a carrier pigeon and it never returned.
2. My fortune cookie said "cook at home."
3. I made a reservation with my fridge instead.
4. I thought "reservation" meant self-doubt.
5. I searched reviews for so long that the restaurant closed, reopened, and changed its menu.
6. I was waiting for the restaurant to call me.
7. I went to call and realized I don't actually know how to make a phone call to a restaurant anymore.
8. I spent so long reading reviews that the restaurant became too intimidating.
9. I assumed the power of positive thinking would secure us a table.
10. My phone autocorrected the restaurant name and I gave up after the third attempt.

CHAPTER 29

Excuses for Being Late Returning a Rental

SERIOUS EXCUSES

1. I assumed the grace period was longer than it turned out to be.
2. Traffic back to the rental location was terrible.
3. I had trouble finding a nearby gas station.
4. I forgot the office closed earlier on weekends.
5. I changed my route and got turned around.
6. I extended another errand and cut it too close.
7. I had to wait for someone else to bring the keys.
8. I tried to top off the tank and ended up at three different gas stations before finding one that worked.
9. I underestimated how long packing the car would take.
10. I didn't factor in the check-in process time.

HUMOROUS EXCUSES

1. The item begged me for "one more day."
2. A time traveler borrowed it.
3. I thought "return date" was optional.
4. I got emotionally attached and needed another day to process the goodbye.
5. I got into a custody battle with my couch.
6. I was teaching it new tricks first.
7. I thought late fees were just suggestions.
8. The item and I formed an emotional attachment I wasn't prepared for.
9. I thought the rental period ran on vibes, not hard deadlines.
10. My sense of time took an unscheduled vacation right at the due date.

CHAPTER 30

Excuses for Losing Your Keys

SERIOUS EXCUSES

1. I set them down while carrying groceries and forgot where.

2. I changed bags and didn't move them over.

3. I dropped them in a jacket pocket and hung it up.

4. I put them somewhere "safe" and can't recall where.

5. I tossed them on a table under a pile of mail.

6. I handed them to someone and didn't take them back.

7. I left them in the door without noticing.

8. I was distracted by a call when I came in.

9. I thought they were in my pocket but they slipped out.

10. I was rushing and didn't use my usual spot.

HUMOROUS EXCUSES

1. A gremlin borrowed them.

2. My keys wanted a vacation.

3. They joined a keychain support group.

4. They eloped with my wallet.

5. I donated them to the "lost and found gods."

6. I put them somewhere logical, which in hindsight was the mistake.

7. They're hiding until I promise to be more organized.

8. My keys took a personal day without filing the paperwork.

9. I set them in a memorable spot that was so memorable I've never found it.

10. My house rearranged itself slightly and threw off my whole system.

CHAPTER 31

Excuses for Avoiding a Neighbor

SERIOUS EXCUSES

1. I was in a rush and couldn't stop to chat.
2. I'd just come home exhausted from work.
3. I was on a call and didn't want to interrupt.
4. I was still fully in work mode and couldn't shift gears fast enough for small talk.
5. I was in house clothes and felt awkward.
6. I had food in the car that needed the fridge.
7. I was late for another commitment.
8. I get anxious with unexpected small talk.
9. I'd had a long day and needed quiet.
10. I didn't notice you until I was already past.

HUMOROUS EXCUSES

1. I timed my exit for a window that seemed clear and then the window closed.
2. I was rehearsing my ninja routine.
3. My blinds declared a strict no-visitor policy.
4. I was incognito as my own twin.
5. I had been talking to people all day and had exactly nothing left.
6. I was teaching myself to be invisible.
7. My introvert card was maxed out.
8. I timed it perfectly every day until the one day I didn't.
9. I became one with the shrubbery and waited it out.
10. I now know every inch of the route from my car to my front door that avoids direct line of sight.

CHAPTER 32

Excuses for Missing a School Event

SERIOUS EXCUSES

1. I couldn't get off work at that time.
2. Traffic near the school was completely backed up.
3. I misread the event time on the notice.
4. I showed up at the right time on the wrong day and had already driven home before I figured it out.
5. A sibling had an overlapping activity.
6. I didn't realize there wouldn't be enough parking.
7. I got the date mixed up with another event.
8. I was waiting on a ride that came too late.
9. I had a health issue flare up that evening.
10. I mixed up which campus the event was on.

HUMOROUS EXCUSES

1. My pencil club held me hostage.
2. I thought "school event" was code for nap time.
3. I was lost in a spelling bee I wasn't competing in.
4. I arrived and couldn't find parking, circled for twenty minutes, and called it a commitment.
5. I mistook it for a pajama day.
6. My homework ate my calendar.
7. I was stuck grading my own performance.
8. My phone sent the reminder to itself and never told me.
9. My carpool forgot me and I took it as a sign from the universe.
10. I thought school events were optional training montages, not mandatory.

CHAPTER 33

Excuses for Forgetting an Anniversary

SERIOUS EXCUSES

1. I confused our date with another important one.
2. I thought we were celebrating on the weekend instead.
3. I didn't check the calendar and trusted my memory.
4. I was buried in a work rush and lost track.
5. I remembered early in the week and then let it slip.
6. I mixed up which month we'd picked to celebrate.
7. I assumed you'd remind me as it got close.
8. I focused on another family event happening that day.
9. I kept meaning to mark it on the calendar and never did.
10. I had a lot of stress and wasn't thinking clearly.

HUMOROUS EXCUSES

1. My reminder ran off with another date.
2. Cupid mixed up the dates for me.
3. I thought anniversaries were biennial.
4. My memory took a romantic day off.
5. My brain outsourced it to next year's me.
6. I celebrated it in my dreams instead.
7. Time played hide and seek with me.
8. I was saving the celebration for when we'd both fully earned it.
9. I had a whole plan and then watched it disappear in real time while doing nothing to stop it.
10. I remembered every anniversary for ten years straight, and this one sensed I was overconfident.

POLLING

CHAPTER 34

Excuses for Not Voting

SERIOUS EXCUSES

1. I missed the registration deadline and couldn't vote.
2. I was out of town and didn't arrange a mail ballot.
3. I didn't receive my ballot in time.
4. I got to the polling place after it closed.
5. I couldn't get a ride there during open hours.
6. Work kept me late and I misjudged timing.
7. I didn't realize the election was that day.
8. I was confused about where I was supposed to go.
9. I had a family emergency and couldn't leave.
10. I felt unprepared and hadn't researched the issues.

HUMOROUS EXCUSES

1. My ballot was stolen by pigeons.
2. I kept waiting for the candidates to deliver the ballot personally.
3. I was busy voting in a video game tournament.
4. I thought "polls" referred to dance class.
5. My civic duty was out of order.
6. I was waiting for the candidates to audition.
7. I thought democracy ran on autopilot.
8. I was waiting for a candidate to come to my door personally.
9. I got in line, checked the time, did some math, and made a decision I still think about.
10. I thought early voting meant I had until the early hours of the next day.

CHAPTER 35

Excuses for Bad Hair Days

SERIOUS EXCUSES

1. I woke up with intense bedhead and limited time.
2. The humidity ruined my styling the moment I left.
3. I ran out of my usual hair products.
4. My shower time got cut short this morning.
5. I tried something new and it didn't work out.
6. My hairdryer stopped working midway.
7. I had to rush out before my hair fully dried.
8. I slept in a weird position and it shows.
9. I had no time to book a much-needed haircut.
10. The wind outside was stronger than I expected.

HUMOROUS EXCUSES

1. My hair joined a rock band overnight.
2. My pillow gave me a new design.
3. My hair was protesting gravity.
4. I was struck by a "fashion tornado."
5. My hair stylist was my pillow.
6. I was auditioning for a scarecrow role.
7. My hair declared independence from styling.
8. My hair held a vote and the result was chaos.
9. I tried three different approaches and my hair rejected all of them diplomatically.
10. My brush and my hair have been in mediation for weeks.

CHAPTER 36

Excuses for Forgetting a Pet Appointment

SERIOUS EXCUSES

1. I mixed the appointment date with another one.
2. I didn't enter it properly in my calendar.
3. I wrote the time on a sticky note that is now living its best life somewhere in this house.
4. I thought the reminder card was for next week.
5. I kept meaning to confirm the time and never did.
6. I was out running errands and lost track of the hour.
7. I confused which pet had which appointment.
8. I misplaced the reminder card from the vet.
9. I had car trouble that morning and forgot to call.
10. I misjudged how far the clinic was from home.

HUMOROUS EXCUSES

1. My dog refused to check the calendar.
2. I mistook "vet" for "bet" and went gambling.
3. The appointment slip became invisible.
4. I set a reminder, the reminder set a reminder, and we both forgot.
5. My pet rescheduled without telling me.
6. I thought pets made their own appointments.
7. My calendar was written in ancient pet hieroglyphs.
8. My pet seemed fine so I assumed no news was good news.
9. I set three reminders, but my phone and I aren't communicating well this month.
10. My vet calendar lives in a drawer that I opened and immediately closed.

CHAPTER 37

Excuses for Not Bringing a Gift

SERIOUS EXCUSES

1. I thought the event didn't require gifts.
2. I planned to bring something and never finished shopping.
3. I ordered a gift that didn't arrive on time.
4. I couldn't decide what was appropriate and stalled.
5. I assumed we'd go in on a group gift.
6. I mixed up the date and missed my chance.
7. I forgot to grab the gift on my way out.
8. I bought something, second-guessed it, returned it, and ran out of time to start over.
9. My budget was tight and I hesitated.
10. I planned to pick something up on the way and couldn't.

HUMOROUS EXCUSES

1. I gift-wrapped my intentions instead.
2. I brought invisible wrapping paper.
3. I thought my presence was the present.
4. Santa borrowed it for a test run.
5. My gift developed stage fright.
6. My gift and I reached the register and had a mutual change of heart.
7. I found the perfect gift online at midnight and by morning had convinced myself it was wrong.
8. I panic-bought something in the parking lot but it didn't survive the walk in.
9. The gift I had in mind existed only in theory.
10. I brought my personality and honestly thought that would be enough.

CHAPTER 38

Excuses for Missing a Family Gathering

SERIOUS EXCUSES

1. I couldn't get the day off from work.
2. Travel costs were higher than I'd expected.
3. A child got sick and I stayed home.
4. My car wasn't reliable enough for the trip.
5. Another family obligation conflicted with the timing.
6. I underestimated how long the drive would take.
7. I realized too late I hadn't booked tickets.
8. I was dealing with personal stress and felt overwhelmed.
9. I misread the date on the family message.
10. The weather made traveling risky that weekend.

HUMOROUS EXCUSES

1. I was kidnapped by a board game marathon.
2. My bag was packed, my shoes were on, and something in my soul said not today.
3. I thought the family tree was out of season.
4. I told myself I'd leave at a specific time and then spent that exact time deciding whether to go.
5. I love this family. I also love them best at a comfortable distance a few times a year.
6. I was stuck in a time loop of getting ready.
7. My family photo wasn't ready for public viewing.
8. I packed, unpacked, repacked, and used up all my available travel energy before leaving the house.
9. My family tree needed pruning and I didn't want to be there for it.
10. My car technically started but seemed very reluctant about the whole trip.

CHAPTER 39

Excuses for Not Watering the Plants

SERIOUS EXCUSES

1. I thought the soil still looked damp enough.
2. I misjudged how often that plant needs water.
3. I was away longer than I planned.
4. I meant to ask someone to water them and forgot.
5. I moved them and stopped seeing them in my routine.
6. I ran out quickly and didn't check them first.
7. I didn't set a reminder like I meant to.
8. I focused more on other chores and overlooked the plants.
9. I confused which day I'd watered them last.
10. I underestimated how hot it would be inside.

HUMOROUS EXCUSES

1. My plants told me they were fasting.
2. I hired a cactus as their mentor.
3. I was waiting for rain indoors.
4. The watering can was on vacation.
5. I thought photosynthesis covered everything.
6. I was teaching them independence.
7. My watering can filed a formal grievance and I'm awaiting the outcome.
8. I pointed at them encouragingly but apparently that doesn't count.
9. My watering schedule exists only in a notebook I've misplaced.
10. They looked at me with such judgment that watering them would have rewarded the behavior.

CHAPTER 40

Excuses for Missing an Exercise Class

SERIOUS EXCUSES

1. I worked later than planned and got out too late.
2. Traffic to the gym was much heavier than usual.
3. I forgot my workout clothes and had to go home.
4. I wasn't feeling well enough to push myself.
5. I talked myself into going, then out of it, then back in, and missed the window during round three.
6. I got anxious about keeping up with the class.
7. I checked the schedule the night before but not the morning of, and they'd changed it.
8. I arrived and couldn't find parking anywhere.
9. I slept through the alarm I set for it.
10. I prioritized another task and ran out of time.

HUMOROUS EXCUSES

1. My running shoes looked at me. I looked at them. We both knew.
2. I sprained my scrolling thumb.
3. I was allergic to sweat that day.
4. My shoes locked themselves in the closet.
5. My couch offered a competing fitness plan.
6. I was saving my energy for important activities.
7. My workout clothes went into hiding.
8. I laced up my shoes and felt that counted as a warm-up and called it there.
9. The gym and I are going through a phase.
10. My fitness app sent me seventeen reminders and somehow I ignored every one.

CHAPTER 41

Excuses for Losing Your Phone

SERIOUS EXCUSES

1. I set it down while paying and walked away.
2. I switched bags and didn't move it over.
3. I left it on a counter and forgot to pick it up.
4. I slipped it into a pocket that I never rechecked.
5. I dropped it between cushions and didn't notice.
6. I lent it briefly and forgot who had it.
7. I left it on silent and couldn't locate it by ringing.
8. I was in a rush and didn't use my usual spot.
9. I put it on a charger I don't usually use.
10. I left it at work when I left in a hurry.

HUMOROUS EXCUSES

1. My phone ran away to join the circus.
2. My voice assistant filed for independence.
3. It was abducted by aliens for research.
4. It fell in love with my TV remote.
5. My phone wanted more attention than my relationships.
6. It went on a digital detox without me.
7. I set it down in a completely sensible spot that no longer makes any sense to me at all.
8. It slipped into a dimension between the couch cushions that scientists can't explain.
9. I last saw it charging but it seems to have walked off on full battery.
10. I retraced every step I took and the phone was apparently on a completely different journey.

CHAPTER 42

Excuses for Not Attending a Class Reunion

SERIOUS EXCUSES

1. I couldn't make the travel arrangements work.
2. I had a family event already scheduled that weekend.
3. Work deadlines made it hard to get away.
4. I waited too long to book a room.
5. I was anxious about seeing everyone again.
6. I wasn't feeling like myself and didn't want to fake it.
7. I bought a ticket, lost it, found it expired, and took that as the universe weighing in.
8. I had health issues and travel wasn't advised.
9. I wasn't sure who was going and hesitated.
10. I was dealing with financial stress at that time.

HUMOROUS EXCUSES

1. I didn't have time to invent a cooler past.
2. My time machine skipped the wrong year.
3. I was undercover as someone else.
4. I spent so long preparing what I would say to people that I exhausted myself before going.
5. I was still practicing my "success story."
6. My high school memories were on backorder.
7. I RSVPd yes, then maybe, then yes again — which in retrospect functioned as a no.
8. I looked at the invitation for thirty seconds and that felt like enough closure.
9. I sent my best wishes and a version of myself that was much younger.
10. My nostalgia and my anxiety held a vote and anxiety won by a landslide.

CHAPTER 43

Excuses for Being Late to Church

SERIOUS EXCUSES

1. Our morning routine took longer than expected.
2. We had trouble getting everyone out the door.
3. I misjudged how long the drive would take.
4. I overslept and rushed the whole morning.
5. I couldn't find something appropriate to wear.
6. The kids needed three outfit changes and a snack negotiation before we could leave.
7. The kids needed extra time to settle down.
8. The parking lot was packed when we arrived.
9. I confused the start time with the later service.
10. I stopped to grab something for the donation box.

HUMOROUS EXCUSES

1. My halo was still charging.
2. I drove past the parking lot, saw the situation, and drove around the block fourteen times.
3. My angel costume got stuck in the dryer.
4. My toast came out as a sign I should stay home.
5. I mistook the service time for "heavenly standard time."
6. My prayers were stuck in traffic.
7. I was waiting for divine intervention to get me ready.
8. The universe presented me with a very slow traffic light and I respected its message.
9. I arrived, found a seat, and only then realized I'd worn two different shoes.
10. I was running on spiritual time, which operates on a slightly different schedule.

CHAPTER 44

Excuses for Avoiding a Job Interview

SERIOUS EXCUSES

1. I started feeling very ill that morning.

2. I had a family emergency I couldn't ignore.

3. I got to the building, sat in the lobby for five minutes, and left before anyone saw me.

4. I couldn't arrange transportation reliably.

5. My anxiety about the interview spiked badly.

6. I realized I wasn't prepared and panicked.

7. I had an unavoidable conflict at my current job.

8. I mixed up the date with another appointment.

9. I wasn't sure about the role and hesitated.

10. I struggled to find the building and gave up.

HUMOROUS EXCUSES

1. My confidence RSVPd yes and my actual self failed to show up in support.

2. I thought it was casual Friday everywhere.

3. I was waiting for my motivational montage to finish.

4. I was stuck rehearsing in front of my mirror.

5. My confidence was running late.

6. I thought they were interviewing me telepathically.

7. My professional persona was out sick.

8. I arrived at the building, read the company name twice, and kept walking.

9. My handshake needed more preparation time.

10. I talked myself into it and then very quickly talked myself back out.

CHAPTER 45

Excuses for Being Late Picking Someone Up

SERIOUS EXCUSES

1. I left later than I meant to and hit traffic.
2. I left on time but every light on that route had a personal agenda.
3. I couldn't find my keys right when I needed to leave.
4. I had to stop for gas unexpectedly.
5. A call at home delayed me more than I planned.
6. I underestimated how long parking would take.
7. I went to the wrong pickup spot first.
8. I got turned around by a detour on the way.
9. I walked out, went back in for something I forgot, forgot what I went back in for, and lost five minutes.
10. I confused your pickup time in my head.

HUMOROUS EXCUSES

1. My car wanted a nap first.
2. I arrived at the meeting point and the meeting point was not where either of us thought it was.
3. My GPS wanted to sightsee.
4. My calendar pranked me with the wrong day.
5. I got lost in my own thoughts.
6. I circled the block so many times I became a local landmark.
7. I was stuck in a parallel parking dimension.
8. I left on time but my car had a different route in mind.
9. Every traffic light sensed my urgency and held a committee meeting.
10. I circled the pickup spot four times without technically being late until the fifth.

JURY
SUMMONS

CHAPTER 46

Excuses for Skipping Jury Duty

SERIOUS EXCUSES

1. I never saw the original summons in the mail.
2. I mixed up the reporting date on the notice.
3. I was out of town and didn't reschedule properly.
4. I had a significant medical issue at the time.
5. I was caring for a family member that week.
6. I had no reliable transportation to the courthouse.
7. My employer couldn't adjust my schedule in time.
8. I misunderstood the instructions about calling in.
9. I was already buried in my own legal and money problems.
10. I didn't realize I needed to respond right away.

HUMOROUS EXCUSES

1. I thought it was a talent show audition.
2. I was busy judging a pie contest.
3. My crystal ball already decided the verdict.
4. I mistook jury duty for jewelry duty.
5. I thought "jury" meant "fury" and ran away.
6. My impartiality was out of order.
7. I was practicing my "objection!" voice.
8. I wrote it on three different calendars and all three let me down.
9. I thought jury duty was like jury suggestion — participation was voluntary.
10. I have very strong opinions and frankly I was protecting the judicial process.

CHAPTER 47

Excuses for Not Volunteering

SERIOUS EXCUSES

1. My work schedule is packed and unpredictable.
2. I'm caring for someone at home most evenings.
3. I don't have reliable transportation to get there.
4. I struggle with social situations and big groups.
5. I'm balancing classes and a job at the same time.
6. I'm dealing with my own health issues right now.
7. I wasn't sure how much time was really required.
8. I felt unqualified for most of the roles.
9. I let my nerves stop me from signing up.
10. I meant to start after things "slowed down."

HUMOROUS EXCUSES

1. I thought "volunteer" meant "volleyball."
2. I read the sign-up sheet three times and each time I closed the tab to think about it more.
3. I spent so long choosing the right role that all the roles were taken by the time I decided.
4. I thought volunteering meant donating pizza.
5. My altruism was in the shop for repairs.
6. I was saving my good deeds for a rainy day.
7. I meant to sign up the week before and the week before that and the week before that.
8. I talked about volunteering so enthusiastically that I think I confused it with actually going.
9. My intentions were excellent. My calendar remained completely blank.
10. My good intentions were fully loaded but my follow-through ran out of fuel.

CHAPTER 48

Excuses for Burning Dinner

SERIOUS EXCUSES

1. I stepped away for what I described to myself as "just a second."
2. I set the heat higher than the recipe said.
3. I misread the cooking time on the instructions.
4. I walked away "for a minute" that became much longer.
5. I used a new pan and didn't adjust the temperature.
6. I tried to cook too many dishes at once.
7. I forgot to set a timer before stepping away.
8. The oven runs hotter than I realized.
9. I didn't stir as often as I needed to.
10. I underestimated how fast it would brown.

HUMOROUS EXCUSES

1. My smoke alarm wanted attention.
2. I thought "burnt" was the new gourmet.
3. I followed a dragon's cookbook by mistake.
4. My food wanted to cosplay as charcoal.
5. I was cooking with passion, not precision.
6. My culinary creativity got out of hand.
7. I thought "blackened" was always intentional.
8. The recipe and I had a creative difference of opinion.
9. I walked away for what felt like thirty seconds and arrived back in a different era.
10. I thought the smoke was the dish announcing it was done.

CHAPTER 49

Excuses for Overspending While Shopping

SERIOUS EXCUSES

1. I found unplanned sales and got carried away.
2. I didn't go in with a firm budget.
3. I treated myself after a stressful week.
4. I convinced myself I'd return what I didn't need.
5. I shopped while hungry and grabbed extras.
6. I used a card instead of cash and lost track.
7. I added "just one more" item too many times.
8. I forgot about upcoming bills when I was there.
9. I followed suggestions from staff without checking prices.
10. I bought gifts on impulse without planning.

HUMOROUS EXCUSES

1. The cart hypnotized me.
2. My wallet sprouted a leak.
3. I was auditioning for Extreme Couponing.
4. The cashier dared me to spend more.
5. I went in for one thing and the store had a very compelling counterargument.
6. I thought money grew on trees in the parking lot.
7. I told myself each item was a treat, and I had apparently earned a lot of treats that week.
8. The store layout was specifically engineered to defeat me and it succeeded.
9. Everything was exactly my size, which felt like a personal invitation.
10. I made a budget but it was more of a suggestion than a rule.

CHAPTER 50

Miscellaneous, Ridiculous, and Legendary Excuses

HUMOROUS EXCUSES

1. My time machine ran out of gas.

2. A raccoon challenged me to karaoke.

3. My parrot became my life coach.

4. I was abducted by clowns.

5. I tripped into a parallel universe.

6. A dragon borrowed my Wi-Fi.

7. My couch declared itself president.

8. I was cursed by a talking potato.

9. A wizard demanded my laundry.

10. My goldfish held a motivational seminar.

11. I was drafted into a penguin parade.

12. My shadow took the day off.

13. My toaster recruited me for its rebellion.

14. I got stuck in a staring contest with the moon.

15. A unicorn blocked my driveway.

16. My alarm clock eloped with my coffee maker.

17. Aliens needed me to judge their dance contest.

18. My houseplants staged a rock concert.

19. I was legally bound by the terms of my streaming agreement.

20. I outsourced my morning routine to my subconscious and it has very different priorities.

21. I signed a contract with procrastination.

And there you have it — 1,001 reasons, alibis, explanations, and creative reframings of the human condition. Whether you used this book as a reference guide, a survival manual, or simply proof that you are not alone in your spectacular failures, the mission is complete. Go forth. Be late. Forget things. Lose your keys. And when someone asks why — you'll know exactly what to say.

www.ingramcontent.com/pod-product-compliance
Lightning Source LLC
LaVergne TN
LVHW010627100826
845148LV00014B/3149
* 9 7 9 8 2 3 4 0 9 6 8 5 2 *